How Can I Help?
Friends Helping Friends™

HELPING A FRIEND IN AN
ABUSIVE RELATIONSHIP

Martin Gitlin

ROSEN
PUBLISHING

New York

Published in 2017 by The Rosen Publishing Group, Inc.
29 East 21st Street, New York, NY 10010

Library of Congress Cataloging-in-Publication Data

Names: Gitlin,Marty, author.
Title: Helping a friend in an abusive relationship / Martin Gitlin.
Description: First edition. | New York : Rosen Publishing, 2017. | Series: How can I help? Friends helping friends | Includes bibliographical references and index.
Identifiers: LCCN 2016017298| ISBN 9781499464382 (library bound) | ISBN 9781499464368 (pbk.) | ISBN 9781499464375 (6-pack)
Subjects: LCSH: Intimate partner violence—Juvenile literature. | Dating violence—Juvenile literature. | Teenagers—Abuse of—Juvenile literature.
Classification: LCC HV6626 .G557 2017 | DDC 362.82/92—dc23
LC record available at https://lccn.loc.gov/2016017298

Manufactured in China

CONTENTS

INTRODUCTION

D o you suspect that your friend is in an abusive relationship?

Your friend could be male or female. Gay or straight. Accepting or unaccepting that he or she is being abused. Yearning to escape the relationship or wishing to continue it. No matter the circumstances, if you

Feeling trapped in an abusive relationship can be a depressing experience, but friends can do much to help.

suspect that your friend is in a dangerous relationship, you know you want to help.

You also know that ignorance can do more harm than good. So learn about the subject and gain an awareness of what your friend is experiencing. To be of any help, study the warning signs of emotional and physical abuse. Acquire an understanding of what constitutes abuse. Only through familiarity with the issue can you properly aid and assist those who are being victimized.

This is scary stuff, and it can be overwhelming and intimidating. However, it's important to know that neither you nor your friend is in this alone. Trusted family members can be loving and caring sources for advice and support. School counselors specialize in guiding students not just with academic problems but personal ones as well. Mental health care professionals provide therapy, which can give the abused the emotional strength to stand up to their abusers and free themselves from the shackles of harmful relationships. The internet is full of advocacy websites and agencies providing knowledge of the issue and paths to an escape. Also, law enforcement officials are available to protect those who fear for their safety. You can learn from all of these resources in gathering information to help your friend.

As a victim of an abusive relationship, your friend is not alone. According to Love Is Respect, nearly 1.5 million high school students across the United States have experienced physical abuse during a one-year period. About 10 percent have been intentionally hit, slapped, or otherwise battered by a boyfriend or girlfriend. One in three adolescents has been the target of physical, sexual, emotional, or verbal abuse from a dating partner. Those numbers exceed the rates of other forms of youth violence.

We all think that such abuse won't happen to our friends or people we know, but statistics prove that we are dangerously mistaken. That is particularly the case for females. According to Love Is Respect, incidents of intimate partner violence among girls and young women between the ages of sixteen and twenty-four are almost triple the national average. Violent behavior can be perpetrated by those as young as twelve years old and often grows more vicious over time. More than one in five teenage girls has been physically or sexually assaulted by a dating partner, according to *USA Today*.

These statistics are powerful, and they can help you understand what your friend is going through. However, awareness of the numbers and love for a victim doesn't make you an expert in the field. Attempting to counsel your friend could do more harm than good. This is a serious matter pertaining to the mental, emotional, and physical health of a friend.

It's important that your friend knows that you care. It's important to provide support, encouragement, and even shelter. Most of all, it's important to guide your friends to seek out professionals trained to help them and to urge them to follow the plans to get them out of their situation. Knowing what's best for your friends is what makes you the best friend you can be.

CHAPTER ONE

HOW CAN YOU TELL?

The first step to helping a friend in an abusive relationship is recognizing how an abusive relationship operates. This is especially difficult when the friend does not recognize the abuse or is unwilling to accept that he or she is indeed a victim.

It doesn't matter if a friend is male or female. Those under the impression that only girls and women are victims of relationship abuse are misguided. According to the National Domestic Violence Hotline, more than one in three women in the United States have experienced physical violence or stalking by an intimate partner, but nearly 30 percent of all men have been similarly victimized. Though about 80 percent of all victims of intimate partner violence from 1994 to 2010 in the United States were female, the number that was male is far too large to be ignored. Intimate partner violence affects more than twelve million Americans every year. These figures do not include more subtle forms of malice that fall into the emotional abuse category, such as intimidation and manipulation.

Those who yearn to help a friend in need should be aware of the many warning signs of an abusive relationship.

WARNING SIGNS

Some signs that a friend is being abused are relatively easy to detect through idle conversation or observation. You may have noticed that your friend's boyfriend or girl-friend insults or puts down your friend in front of oth-ers, leading to public shame. Many victims accept such insults, which in turn weak-ens their self-respect. It's good to let your friend know that you don't like the way he or she is being treated. Let your friend know you want to help her. However, you need to do this in a supporting way rather than in harsh terms that could make your friend feel bad about the relationship.

Friends of a victim might also notice that he or she is being controlled, which is one form of emotional abuse. Perhaps your friend's boyfriend or girlfriend has determined which friends he can see, how she should dress, where he can go, or in what activities she can participate. Abusers use such tactics to feel a sense of power in a relationship.

They seek to force their partners to act the way they want them to act. This might include the use of alcohol or drugs. They might attempt to coerce a partner to become sexually active with them. They might even use physical intimidation with guns, knives, or other weapons to exert control in a relationship.

Your friend could be intimidated or shamed enough to keep the abuse secret. It is possible he or she feels that having a partner is so important that opening up to another person would jeopardize the relationship. Friends don't have to suspect a problem exists to investigate one. True friends observe, listen, and pick up clues that could lead them to suspect there is a problem. They should speak with counselors or relationship abuse experts to learn more. Even simply asking your friend how his relationship is going can reveal through body language and verbal hints that he needs help.

Look for signs of emotional abuse. Perhaps you have noticed that your friend seems overeager to please a partner. He or she might unquestionably go along with anything the boyfriend or girlfriend says or does. Maybe your friend feels the need to constantly check in with his or her partner by phone or text. Or your friend no longer partakes in activities for which he or she has shown a passion, in order to spend more time with a significant other. A relationship is healthiest when both people are free of fear and can grow both separately and together.

Anyone who knows and understands their friend's personality should be able to identify changes that may provide evidence of emotional abuse. A usually outgoing friend

LEARNING ABOUT ABUSE THROUGH POETRY

Young actress Sarah Hyland has gained fame through her performance on the highly successful and acclaimed sitcom *Modern Family*. She also gained unwanted fame by receiving a restraining order against boyfriend Matt

Prokop after he physically and emotionally abused her to the extent that she said she feared for her life.

Hyland remained fairly quiet about the matter, hoping to move on to a new chapter in her life. But she did open up about it to talk show host Meredith Viera about a month after filing legal documents to keep Prokop

Young actress Sarah Hyland was victimized in one of the more publicized cases of relationship abuse, but she gained inspiration through poetry and took action to free herself.

away. Hyland spoke about the inspiration she received from poetry, showing that one can find encouragement in a variety of sources.

"There were two quotes that I want to say," she told Viera. "One is a Dylan Thomas poem: 'Do not go gentle into that good night. Rage, rage against the dying of the light,' which is one of my favorite poems. It just strikes a chord with me. And then also Robert Frost. 'The only way out is through.' People have to go through things in order to become the person they are today."

might have become withdrawn. His or her confidence might have drained away. A friend might seem depressed or anxious and speak about the futility of school or life in general.

There might also be noticeable signs of physical abuse, like bruises. Victims of physical abuse often wear clothing that hides scars or bruises. This clothing can be suspicious, such as long-sleeved shirts in the summertime and sunglasses indoors. Frequent absences from school or work could indicate physical abuse as well.

As a friend, you can also look for other forms of relationship abuse. Abusive partners often seek to control spending habits and impose other restrictions on their boyfriends or girlfriends. If your friend's partner has discouraged your friend from buying something he or she wanted or from going to an anticipated event, a red flag should be raised. Why would someone who loves your friend want to disappoint him or her like that?

11

DON'T GOSSIP

Gossiping and using social media to spread the word about a friend can prove harmful and even dangerous to his or her relationship.

It's important to remember that this delicate situation should remain private at this point. It might be tempting to share your thoughts and concerns with other friends in person or via text and email.

At this point in the process, your victimized friend is unaware of your fears. He or she must learn about your concerns only through you. If you need to share your concerns, do so through confidential conversations with counselors and professionals specializing in relationship abuse. They can provide insight on whether your friend has indeed been victimized.

It is particularly harmful if your friend discovers your suspicions on social media sites such as Facebook or various chats. The bond of trust would then be broken before you even got a chance to help. Imagine how betrayed your friend would feel after finding out that you initiated a thread about his or her relationship for everyone to see on the internet. This could make your friend cling tighter to the abuser. The tactic could also prove more dangerous if the abusive part-ner perceives it as a threat to the control he or she has over your friend.

YOU CAN ONLY DO SO MUCH

It's important to understand that the only people that should be involved at any point, aside from yourself, are the victim, trusted adult family members, and professionals such as counselors, health care providers, relationship abuse spe-cialists, and law enforcement officials. It is also important to understand the process. A friend helping a friend can learn from professional experts, but it's up to the victim to get the professionals involved. You can, however, help convince your abused friend to use all the resources available to him or her to find the ideal solution to the problem.

Once you're suspicious of abuse, it's time to communi-cate your feelings to the victim in a supportive fashion. You should hint that you're worried he or she is being abused but don't judge your friend, even if your friend claims he or she is fine and wants to remain in the relationship. One should express an understanding that it is difficult to talk about abuse, but let friends know that you are always available to help whenever it is needed.

"You can say things like, 'I care about you. I'm con-cerned. I'm here for you. Is everything OK? Do you want to talk about anything?'" explains Katie Ray-Jones, who serves as the chief executive officer of the National Domestic Vio-lence Hotline. "If you've noticed specific changes, point them

The support of a group of friends is important in the process of helping a person escape or improve an abusive relationship.

out. 'I do not see you as much as I used to. I noticed that your partner gets upset if you do not answer your phone. Your partner seems to get really upset when you talk to guys at school.' If you feel that they are in danger then you may need more direct language. 'I am concerned; I've noticed bruises. Is everything OK? Is there anything that you need?'"

What your friend requires more than anything is a sounding board, someone who will listen. This can't be achieved in a hectic or noisy environment. Find a quiet place that breeds confidentiality, at a time that's best for both parties and that promises no interruptions. Approach your friend through non-confrontational conversations beginning with a simple question that doesn't directly raise the issue of the abusive relationship. Stating an awareness that a friend seems to be stressed out or a bit down emotionally could open him or her up to sharing concerns about a boyfriend or girlfriend.

When that line of communication has been opened, a victim of relationship abuse will be more likely to trust a friend's judgment. Even a victim who shuts down will now know that the friend cares and will be more likely to question the relationship despite having previously failed to admit the existence of abuse.

It has been said that you catch more flies with honey than you do with vinegar. That old expression is particularly apt in this case. Those who show they care through kindness are far more likely to gain success helping their friend than those who show they care through anger or judgment.

CHAPTER TWO

TAKING THE NEXT STEP

Maybe you will be lucky. Maybe your friend will admit immediately he or she has a problem and will take every step necessary to solve it.

But maybe not. Friends helping friends are often met with some level of resistance along the way. Perhaps the victim will claim that no such abuse exists in a relationship with a boyfriend or girlfriend. Or that despite evidence or incidents of mistreatment, the abuser has a wonderful heart and can change. Or even that the friend seeking to help is jealous of the relationship and trying to unjustly break it up.

A subject as personal as dating can elicit a wide range of responses, including anger and resentment. What's important for you to understand is that you shouldn't be sucked into that emotional roller coaster. Instead, your positive support should be unwavering. Listen to your friend rather than react. Try to help rather than make judgments. Even if it seems that the decision of a friend is final, and he or she will continue to maintain what you strongly suspect is an abusive relationship, you shouldn't judge. That will only batter a self-image that has already been weakened by the relationship, driving your friend away from help and closer to the abuser.

Most critical is that you not belittle your friend. He or she might put up a stoic front, but victims of abusive relationships have already lost a level of self-respect. Accusing a friend of being weak for yearning to stay with a boyfriend or girlfriend despite the negative consequences can only damage a battered ego further. You're not a professional therapist. Anything that could prove damaging to your friend psychologically should be avoided. You must provide support, and putdowns will have the opposite effect.

A negative approach to communication is not an effective way to open oneself up to admitting there is a problem and taking steps to fix it.

FOCUS ON THE POSITIVE

Friends helping friends shouldn't give up even if they feel like they are talking to a wall. Maybe the initial conversation with your friend didn't bring about the desired result, which is an admission that he or she is in an abusive relationship and an expressed desire to escape. There are supportive ways, however, to show concern for a friend while raising his or her level of self-respect and self-reliance.

Among them is encouragement to partake in activities with friends and family members away from the abuser. Those close to your friend can provide positive reinforcement through the enjoyment of their company. They might or might not be aware that their friend or sister or brother is in an abusive relationship. What's most important is that the experience will help the victim improve his or her self-image.

Another way to help your friend without forcing the issue is to allow him or her to gain an understanding of what a healthy dating relationship should entail. You can do this by planning activities that include couples your age who

Experiencing the joys of friendships and healthy relationships can help an abused friend gain an understanding about his or her own negative relationship.

are enjoying a happy and nonabusive existence. It should be a partnership in which both people have been given the freedom to grow separately and the time to embrace platonic relationships with others. Your friend could take a step forward by experiencing what a thriving relationship looks like and comparing it to the one in which he or she is currently involved. This can be achieved without suspecting an ulterior motive if an activity with a couple in a healthy relationship is planned, and he or she can witness how they interact.

ABUSE IN A SPOTLIGHT

Pop singer Rihanna didn't suffer physical abuse from fellow musical artist Chris Brown for all to see at first. Then an attack become public knowledge, causing a furor in the entertainment industry. It was one incident that brought relationship abuse into the spotlight.

Rihanna was left bruised and bloody after Brown punched and choked her in a car in 2009. It took months after Brown was arrested for Rihanna to speak about the abuse publicly. She revealed that her father had also been an abuser and that she had vowed never to date one. When the attack was happening, she kept wondering when it was going to stop. She added that she would eventually become happy it happened to her because, as a celebrity, she could use the experience to help young girls with similar relationship issues.

HELPING A FRIEND IN AN ABUSIVE RELATIONSHIP

Positive comparisons can be critical in modern times. Reports of relationship abuse abound in this new era of social media. Teenagers often perceive such behavior among celebrities as normal and therefore accept it in their own partnerships. For instance, many teens of both genders believe it is acceptable for girls to hit boys. And when Chris Brown was revealed to be a physical abuser of fellow singer Rihanna, dating violence expert Emilio Ulloa, who researches the subject for San Diego State University, noted that many high school students believed the latter had likely done something to deserve it. However, the fact is nobody deserves to be abused.

Singer Rihanna (*right*) received tremendous attention when her abusive relationship with boyfriend Chris Brown (*left*) was revealed to the public.

CONTROL IS NOT LOVE

Those who believe that dating violence is acceptable based on what they hear or read are far more likely to allow it in their own lives. Teens should understand that no form of abuse—mental, emotional or physical—should be tolerated. When they understand this, they should try to help their friends understand. Your friend should know that controlling behavior from a boyfriend or girlfriend shouldn't be misinterpreted as a sign of love. You can help him or her understand this not by lecturing but by expressing how much you and others treasure your friend. Hearing how much he or she means to you can help boost your friend's self-image.

Comfort and support go hand-in-hand with understanding. It's possible that your friend grew up in an abusive relationship at home and might therefore be more accepting of similar treatment in his or her own life. You must also be aware that a lack of love and approval from your friend's parents or other family members might have resulted in a strong desire to maintain a relationship in which love and acceptance is perceived but may not actually exist.

KNOWLEDGE BRINGS UNDERSTANDING

You have likely been close enough to your friend to have gained a thorough understanding of how he or she has been shaped by life experiences. You have also learned enough about his or her current relationship to suspect strongly that your friend has been abused. It is also important that you

21

learn as much as possible about relationship abuse and the mind-set and motivation of abusers to speak intelligently. For instance, abusers tend to escalate their behavior over time. They do not abuse subconsciously. They abuse for selfish reasons. Abuse can't and shouldn't be blamed on such outside influences as drugs, alcohol, financial struggles, depression, jealousy, or the actions of the victim. Abusers might try to placate a boyfriend or girlfriend by apologizing, but that is merely a form of manipulation.

It's important that you become educated not only about the personal relationship of your friend but also about the subject of relationship abuse overall. Compare what you know about your friend's relationship with the facts about relationship abuse that you learn from internet research, as well as conversations with counselors and local domestic violence agencies.

It's important that you not use this knowledge in a confrontational way, even if you believe through an initial discussion that your friend doesn't feel like a victim. What a victim claims must be accepted as truth. Listen without judging. Your friend might have talked himself or herself into believing that everything is fine while feeling a sense of shame and inadequacy. Expressing disbelief in the story can be counterproductive even if you sense that your friend is defending the abuser and the relationship to secure emotional protection. After all, those who are controlled by their partners often really believe all is well. They can't help themselves until they truly believe the relationship isn't right. You can't force your friend to change or leave the relationship. He or she has been robbed of power in his or her relationship by an abuser. That power must be restored before positive steps are taken. Until then, you must validate your friend's feelings and encourage self-empowerment.

Self-empowerment doesn't translate into dealing with the situation alone. Quite the opposite! Your job is to encourage your friend to seek out and embrace the advice of those who focus professionally on helping young people in abusive relationships. You might convince your friend that he or she should keep an open mind and talk to a professional, even if he or she comes away believing the relationship is solid. The key is to get your friend to enlist help from an expert. Remember, you're not an expert, but you may have found someone who is. In any case, your mission is far from over.

MYTHS AND FACTS

MYTH: Victims have types of personalities that accept and even encourage abuse.

FACT: Many studies have confirmed that there is no set personality trait that describes the abused. The abuser alone is responsible.

MYTH: Incidents of relationship violence are usually the result of a momentary loss of temper.

FACT: It is quite the opposite. The abuser makes a conscious decision to batter and stores up anger and frustration during the course of the day to take out on the victim.

MYTH: Males are rarely the victims in abusive relationships.

FACT: Twenty percent of all victims of intimate partner violence from 1994 to 2010 in the United States were male.

CHAPTER THREE

STAYING ON BOARD THE FRIENDSHIP

Nobody who steadfastly refuses to be helped can be helped. But a victim of relationship abuse most assuredly wants to better his or her life. The commitment of a friend should not end if the first conversations reveal an initial unwillingness to accept support or an insistence that the relationship with a boyfriend or girlfriend is perfectly healthy.

The first step to breaking the ice is one that doesn't force the involvement of outsiders. You can start simply by pointing your friend to the internet. There are many websites that focus on teenagers

Reflective moments allow friends to give thought and learn about the most effective ways to help those in abusive relationships.

and provide information about relationship abuse; this can help your friend become aware that he or she is a victim and that there's nothing to be ashamed about. The anonymity and relatively low pressure of reading information on the internet is a good way to begin to help your friend.

FIRST STOP: THE INTERNET

Among these great resources is Love Is Respect (http://loveisrespect.org), which compares and contrasts healthy and unhealthy relationships. It stresses that both parties in a thriving partnership can speak their minds and voice their concerns freely and fearlessly. It cites that mutual respect is a cornerstone of a healthy relationship and that compromise is a key to ending disagreements fairly. The site also points out the importance of building confidence rather than shattering it through insults and putdowns. It highlights the need for both partners to establish and live within boundaries that allow them to spend time separately hanging out with friends, partaking in cherished activities, and keeping email and social media passwords private. Love Is Respect also provides a list and details of support systems and features quizzes that can enlighten readers as to the nature of the relationship and provide an understanding about the possibility that the abuser is capable of change.

Another insightful website is Start Strong (http://startstrongteens.org), which is associated with the Futures Without Violence program. The site specifically targets middle school students. It seeks to plant the seeds of success by educating those who have probably not begun dating yet about the keys to creating healthy relationships. Start Strong works to empower kids and help them build strong self-images at a young age so that they can more easily transfer those positive traits into eventual dating partnerships. The result is fewer abusers, fewer victims, and more teens who can recognize abuse when confronted with it.

Yet another site worthy of attention is Teens Experiencing Abusive Relationships (http://teensagainstabuse.org). Particularly relevant are pages titled "Is My Friend a Victim?" and "Escaping Bad Relationships." The first lists signs of an abusive situation that could cement suspicions and awaken a friend to the realization that he or she is a victim, such as fear of displeasing a partner or not enjoying once-cherished activities. The second cites a four-step process for breaking the shackles of an abusive relationship that can be of help to a friend after he or she decides to break free.

Teens Experiencing Abusive Relationships also features a pie chart that allows a friend that has admitted to victimization to determine what level of abuse he or she has reached. The "Cycle of Abuse" has four stages. The first is the green stage, in which both partners are happy and the relationship is enjoyable and fulfilling. Cracks in the relationship begin forming in the yellow stage as the abuser displays a level of frustration, and small arguments start ensuing. The victim begins trying to placate and calm the abuser while spending more time with the boyfriend or girlfriend and less with others. The victim in the yellow stage is unsuccessful in his or her efforts as disagreements turn into screaming matches in which the abuser blames everything on the victim.

27

What has been termed "the Cycle of Abuse" often includes physical battering by boyfriends and girlfriends.

The most dangerous level in the cycle is the red stage. It is the shortest and most harmful. It can be triggered by one incident that leads to physical violence, public humiliation, or even the use of weapons.

The victim often finds the courage at this stage to contact authorities and leave the abuser. But quite often neither party works to make the separation permanent, which leads back to the green stage. The abuser apologizes, buys a gift such as flowers for the victim as a token of sincerity, and promises he or she will change. The victim agrees, dropping all attempts to punish the abuser in the hopes of a peaceful and lasting outcome. The abuser quite often has learned nothing from the experience, and the cycle begins anew.

FAME, FORTUNE, AND RELATIONSHIP ABUSE

All seemed well for young actress, director, and singer Debby Ryan. The former Disney star's career was thriving, but little did fans know that she was being victimized in a relationship that hit all the cycles of abuse. At age twenty-two, she spoke about the demons she had been battling in trying to save a relationship that was not worthy of saving.

"Love is freaking hard, and fighting for a relationship is so much work and can be so beautiful, and if you're going to fight so hard for something that does not make you stronger and better and build you up, something's wrong," she said. "I got to the point of being grabbed, being locked out of rooms, being screamed at, having things thrown at me, cussed at, begged for forgiveness, cried to, all while trying to keep it together and justifying this relationship. And that was the point that I realized maybe there was a red flag … I'm very fortunate because I had people help me get this person out of my life, out of my house—like physically lock the door."

Ryan then sought to help others fighting relationship abuse. She began working with Mary Kay cosmetics and Love Is Respect for the "Don't Look Away" campaign, which raises awareness about abuse in teen dating relationships.

You can gain knowledge from these sites that allows you to speak more expertly with your friend about past issues contributing to his or her current situation. Keep in mind, however, that you are not a mental health care professional. Though these sites can help explain why your friend might be allowing or even accepting abuse, you are in no position to analyze his or her emotional state on your own.

Such a scenario can be discussed with your friend if he or she is open to it. But rather than attempt to decipher where the relationship in question fits into the cycle, it's better to gently steer your friend into conversations with trusted loved ones or counselors. Once your friend expresses an openness to seeking help, you can suggest in a non-lecturing manner that specialists can better judge what is a healthy relationship and what might be destructive. You've already gained knowledge of bonds between your friend and specific family members, the form of mistreatment (physical or emotional) being dealt out by the boyfriend or girlfriend, and the current stage your friend has reached in the cycle of abuse. Now you can propose the most logical and potentially helpful alternatives.

WHOM TO TURN TO FOR SUPPORT

Perhaps, based on your understanding of your friend's family, you feel that the love and caring of his or her parent would provide the best path. Maybe you feel that your friend's older sibling would be a better source of logical advice. Or maybe your friend's parents or siblings are part of the problem and could present a roadblock to your friend's progress. If that's the case, suggest your friend meet with a guidance counselor at school or a local domestic violence agency that provides counseling or support groups. The latter is particularly inviting because it allows your friend to interact with and

Support groups that help victims of relationship abuse can be found through many avenues, including in schools and on the internet.

learn from others who are experiencing the same problems without making the issue known to classmates or others.

Physical abuse raises another set of issues and options. If you have become aware that a friend has been threatened with physical abuse or has already been victimized, you will need to take a more aggressive approach, such as contacting domestic abuse hotlines or law enforcement officials.

This step is part of a safety net that allows your friend to escape what has become a dangerous situation and will be discussed in depth in the following section.

In the end, however, you must realize that the victim—your friend—bears the ultimate responsibility. Though it's difficult and even painful to watch someone close to you get hurt emotionally or physically, your friend must be allowed to take charge of his or her own life. Support is important, but it must remain steadfast even if a friend decides to remain in what you strongly believe to be an abusive relationship.

You won't be able to change your friend's mind on your own. Action into which a victim is unwillingly pushed will likely not be permanent. Your friend must change before he or she can change his or her life. And that will require the advice and work of those trained to aid teenagers in abusive relationships.

CHAPTER FOUR

SETTING UP A SAFETY NET

Your friend has been falling. Now it's time to help set up a safety net. That's a personalized and practical plan that allows people in abusive relationships to remain unharmed before and after they escape. It also brings into play those best suited to aid the victim depending on the level and form of abuse.

It doesn't take you out of the picture. You should never give up on the situation or refuse to take your friend seriously even when he or she is making claims about the relationship that seem ridiculous. It takes persistence to help a friend in need, and the importance of your work should not be downplayed in your own mind. It's your job to help your friend make potentially life-changing decisions. That begins with continuous emotional support.

STEPPING BACK, BUT NOT AWAY

One must validate the feelings of a victim even if they are not understood. This means that, even after you've found help for your friend, you should remain a trusted sounding board who always listens and never judges. It's impossible to avoid developing personal opinions about what a friend should do, but it's dangerous to allow those judgments to seep into conversations with your friend. Leave advice beyond seeking counsel to experts in the field of relationship abuse. For example, your gut reaction might be to criticize your friend's abuser, but that could drive your friend back into his or her arms. It is far more productive to express concern in a comforting way about unhealthy aspects of your friend's relationship.

Those who express a desire to leave an abusive relationship should be praised. You should definitely tell your friend that you support him or her no matter what.

There are many ways to help the abused, but simply letting your friend know that you are there to help and that you care is an important first step.

State that it takes courage and strength to make such a bold move. Tell your friend that you have learned a lot about relationship abuse from specialists in the field. Now it's time for your friend to confide in others such as parents, teachers, counselors, religious leaders, or even law enforcement officials. Remember that you are not tattling on anyone. You're trying to save a cherished person.

Those helping a victim of relationship abuse must remember that they represent a significant part of the safety net for a vulnerable friend. They can make suggestions that do not require professional experience and training. They can urge the friend to partake in activities that make him or her feel good, such as sports or theater or school clubs.

They can invite the victim to movies or concerts. If the friend has yet to make a commitment to break away from the abuser, such fun activities will allow him or her to compare the positive and carefree feelings received with the stressful emotional state that the relationship brings. The abuser has probably brought such emotions as sadness, loneliness, and even anger into the life of the victim. Friends can bring joy, comradeship, and peace of mind. You can still provide your friend with support and friendship as he or she receives help from experts.

Another important thing to remember is that you can help your friend find time away from the abuser, but you can't permanently keep that person out of the picture. Only law enforcement officials given proof of abuse can take steps to make that happen.

THE CLOTHESLINE PROJECT

One unique way to help raise awareness about violence against women is to participate in the Clothesline Project. The program was launched in 1990 in Cape Cod, Massachusetts. It began as a vehicle for women affected by domestic violence to express their emotions, but it can also be used by anyone to make a statement against relationship violence.

The Clothesline Project asks people to decorate a shirt in any way that expresses feelings about violence against women. The artists then hang the shirt outside on a clothesline to be viewed by anyone passing through. The shirts served at first as testimony to the problem of violence against women in American society. However, the efforts of those backing the Clothesline Project helped it reach a global scale.

Your friend should know that the National Domestic Violence Hotline urges victims to maintain evidence of physical abuse such as photos of injuries and journals chronicling violent incidents and threats.

A HELPFUL WORKBOOK

The website Love Is Respect features a safety guide for teenagers seeking to escape an abusive relationship. Your friend can use its safety workbook, which provides helpful routines

A safety workbook provided by Love Is Respect can provide knowledge and guidance for those experiencing relationship abuse.

that can be critical in keeping him or her emotionally and physically sound on a daily basis.

Among the suggestions are keeping contact with a trusted adult at all times, staying away from isolated places and never walking around alone, avoiding all verbal contact with the abuser, and calling 911 if a dangerous situation arises. Victims can also seek a protective order to serve to legally ensure that the abuser stays away.

The workbook provides space to write down the phone numbers of trusted emergency contacts such as family members and friends, as well as law enforcement agencies, local domestic violence organizations, and even youth shelters. It features a checklist of school officials such as counselors, coaches, teachers, administrators, and security personnel that the abused can count on to be available in case he or she needs a safe haven. It allows a victim to list actions that can be taken to maintain safety in social situations. Among the helpful hints are ensuring that friends they are hanging out with keep their cell phones handy at all times in case they get separated and a dangerous situation occurs. The victim can also be sure to avoid going to malls, restaurants, and stores usually frequented by the abuser.

Several checklists in the workbook serve as constant reminders that you and others are available to help. It provides spaces to write down names and phone numbers of those to call both during an emergency and if he or she is simply depressed or frightened, as well as lines in which to place information for such essential contacts as the National Teen Violence Dating Hotline, local domestic violence organizations, and local free legal assistance agencies.

You should stress to your friend that there's much to be aware of when seeking to remain safe as he or she breaks the bonds of an abusive relationship. The workbook allows victims to list critical considerations such as keeping a cell phone with important phone numbers handy at all times, making certain a trusted adult always knows their whereabouts, staying out of isolated places, and keeping windows

Times of reflective thought can help the abused
consider the best methods to keep themselves safe
from an abusive partner.

and doors locked when they are home alone. They should never speak to the abuser unless it is absolutely necessary—and if it's unavoidable, he or she should make sure others are around. The abused should never stray from home alone at night.

Even the physical safety behind locked and closed doors at home can be dangerous when online. The workbook stresses that victims of relationship abuse shouldn't write anything online he or she would not express in person. Only parents and guardians should have access to passwords. Threatening or abusive texts, emails, and posts from the abuser should be saved. Your friend should have access at home to caller identification, which allows him or her to block harassing phone calls. If contact from the abuser does not stop, your friend should change his or her usernames, email addresses, and cell phone number. It is essential that the victim cut off all personal contact with the abuser.

It is your duty to help your friend follow the workbook guidelines. He or she should make a copy or two for you and a trusted adult. Many victims tend to fall back into the green stage explained on the Teens Experiencing Abusive Relationships website cited previously. You shouldn't try to analyze why your friend seems to be slipping back into the clutches of an apologetic abuser. You're not trained in such psychology and shouldn't use it to nudge your friend back on the right path. You should instead urge him or her to speak with a counselor, mental health professional, or relationship abuse specialist such as those provided by the National Domestic Violence Hotline. Your concern is understandable if your friend appears to be retreating, but advice from an untrained individual such as yourself can do more harm than good.

One should understand, however, that a return to a potentially still-abusive relationship is not the only negative action that can be taken by victims. There are others that can lead to grave danger as well.

CHAPTER FIVE

WHAT TO DO AND WHAT NOT TO DO

W hen you have a friend in an abusive relationship, you must serve as his or her advocate. You should help him or her decide what not to do as well as determine which is the best course of action to take. One action that should never be taken is inaction.

Doing nothing is especially common among males, despite the fact that one in seven have experienced severe physical violence by an intimate partner, according to National Domestic Violence Hotline chief executive officer Katie Ray-Jones. She reports that only 5 percent of callers, chatters, and texters who reach out to the hotline and the Love Is Respect site are male. And only one in four of them stated that they were in an abusive relationship.

"Male victims typically underreport their experiences because they may feel embarrassed or ashamed," Ray-Jones says. "This stems from how American society has defined masculinity. Male victims' experiences are often similar to those of female victims. Male victims report verbal abuse and physical abuse, as well as many of the same controlling

Though fleeing can be tempting for those in abusive relationships, it is no permanent solution and can be quite dangerous both physically and emotionally.

behaviors reported by female victims. However, research shows that the physical abuse experienced by female victims at the hands of a male results in more injuries, and the physical force is more excessive."

ABUSE BY THE NUMBERS

Mary Kay cosmetics has teamed with Love Is Respect to analyze awareness of domestic violence issues in the United States. They take an annual survey to determine whether the issue is growing stronger or weaker in the American consciousness.

The survey revealed that awareness of domestic violence is on the rise. It also demonstrated a level of optimism among young people that it can be eradicated. Half of those in the millennial generation thought that it could be eliminated. The survey also indicated that people believe more education about healthy relationships can make a difference.

Results of the survey showed that nearly one-third of respondents have either experienced domestic abuse personally or seen it happen to someone they know. More than 70 percent expressed confidence that they would know how to react if a domestic abuse case became known to them. But only half say they would intervene if someone they knew was in a verbally or physically abusive relationship.

"It is heartening to see that Americans are becoming more aware and invested in the issue of domestic violence," said Brian Pinero, who serves as chief programs officer at the National Domestic Violence Hotline and Love Is Respect. "However, many are still struggling to recognize the signs of abuse and more education is needed to ensure that adults and teens are building healthy relationships."

AVOIDING AWKWARD ENCOUNTERS

Whether a friend is male or female, gay or straight, one must work to keep him or her away from the abuser. Be aware that sometimes obstacles need to be cleared. Among them can be when the abused shares a class in school with the abuser. In such cases, a conversation should be urged with the teacher, counselor, or school administrator. Knowledge of the nature of the relationship will spur action and likely aid the separation of the abuser and victim.

The abuser and victim might also be members of after-school clubs or sports teams. If that happens, there are a few options for dealing with the situation. One is simply to quit the activity, but that should be discouraged. After all, partaking in enjoyable pursuits is therapeutic and a potentially wonderful diversion for victims of relationship abuse. A second option, which should be encouraged, is to talk with coaches or club supervisors.

The adult can take whatever steps are necessary to keep your friend safe within the school environment. A third possibility is to apply for a restraining order against the abuser. That will not place victim and abuser in separate schools, but it will allow the school to change class and lunch schedules, as well as locker assignments, to force separation. The school can also provide staff and services to address the needs of the victim. By gaining awareness of the abuse, a school will be motivated to notify law enforcement officials if the abuser has violated the restraining order.

DON'T LET YOUR FRIEND RUN AWAY

Sometimes nothing seems to be working for your friend. You sense that he or she might simply run away, which is a very dangerous response to relationship abuse. Running away can be recommended for adults living with abusive partners, or even considered as a last resort for teenagers experiencing physical abuse at home and feeling trapped and endangered. However, it shouldn't be an option for a teenage victim of relationship abuse. Friends might believe they have provided or suggested far too many protective paths for running away to be considered, including experts in the field, caring friends and family members, time spent away from the abuser, and a safety workbook guide. Still, they should be aware of danger signals that indicate the abused might indeed contemplate fleeing.

Among these warning signs that your friend is in danger of running away are dramatic mood swings, problems with school attendance or behavior, giving away clothing or other valuables, asking you to carry his or her money, and asking such questions as, "Do you think anyone would miss me if I leave home?" It will help if you gain an understanding of what life on the street entails for teenagers before you approach your friend with concerns. After all, homeless teenagers are far more likely to be victims of crime and sexual abuse. Runaways have significantly higher rates of depression and alcohol and drug abuse. Girls who flee are more likely to get pregnant. You can tell these things to your friend and hopefully stop him or her from taking off.

Literally running away from relationship abuse is never a solution. Those that suspect a friend is considering bolting should encourage him or her to talk to a school counselor or relationship abuse specialist such as the National Domestic Violence Hotline. Perhaps they can offer lodging at their home for a couple of days. That would serve to confuse the abuser as to his or her whereabouts, leading to a greater feeling of comfort and security. It would also provide time to convince your friend to embrace more positive options than running away.

STAY SAFE

Frustration and concern for your friend might lead you to consider confronting his or her abuser. It is important to reject such impulses. The result might not only be counterproductive, but also dangerous. Ray-Jones stresses that it should definitely be avoided. "Focus on your friend, not the abusive partner," she says. "Even if your friend stays with their partner, it's important they still feel comfortable talking to you about it. Don't badmouth the abuser to your friend nor others. Don't contact their abuser or publicly post negative things about them online. It'll only worsen the situation for your friend...The abusive partner may begin to isolate your friend from you."

That last point is particularly important. A friend can only remain a positive influence if he or she is trusted and available. Involving the abuser in a plan to help a friend escape an abusive relationship saps your power and potentially weakens the victim. Awakening the abuser to outside influences could also prove dangerous to everyone involved.

WHAT TO DO AND WHAT NOT TO DO

You are on a selfless mission. You are seeking to help someone in need and quite possibly in danger. But your goal is not to wrest your friend away from the abuser so he or she will be free to spend more time with you. Your primary task is to ensure that your friend receives the help he or she needs from those trained in aiding teens in abusive relationships. Don't allow your ego to interfere. Only then can your friend take steps onto the path to freedom and happiness.

10 GREAT QUESTIONS TO ASK A GUIDANCE COUNSELOR

1 SHOULD I ASK MY FRIEND TO COME IN AND SPEAK WITH YOU EVEN IF I'M NOT YET SURE IT IS AN ABUSIVE RELATIONSHIP?

2 WHAT ARE THE MOST TELLING CLUES THAT MY FRIEND IS BEING EMOTIONALLY ABUSED?

3 WHAT SCHOOL ACTIVITIES CAN BE RECOMMENDED TO ALLOW MY FRIEND TO REGAIN LOST SELF-ESTEEM?

Strong self-esteem free of abuse is essential to those yearning to enjoy their teenage years.

4 SHOULD PARENTS BE NOTIFIED THAT I SUSPECT RELATIONSHIP ABUSE?

5 WHAT CAN THE SCHOOL DO TO KEEP THE COUPLE SEPARATE IF MY FRIEND WANTS TO ESCAPE THE RELATIONSHIP?

6 HAVE WE REACHED THE POINT WHERE I SHOULD SPEAK WITH LOCAL DOMESTIC VIOLENCE SPECIALISTS?

7 HOW WOULD YOU CONVINCE MY FRIEND TO TAKE ACTION?

8 HOW CAN EMOTIONAL ABUSE BE MORE HARMFUL TO MY FRIEND THAN PHYSICAL ABUSE?

9 WHAT IS THE BEST WAY TO ENSURE THAT MY FRIEND DOESN'T RUN AWAY?

10 WHICH TEACHER AT SCHOOL COULD BEST HELP MY FRIEND?

GLOSSARY

ADVOCACY Work for the benefit of a person or cause.

BELITTLE To put someone down in an attempt to weaken him or her emotionally.

COERCE To compel by force or physical or emotional intimidation to get one's way.

CONFIDENTIALITY Keeping something secret between two or more individuals.

DIVERSION A tactic to keep a person's mind off the subject at hand.

EMPOWER To strengthen another person mentally or emotionally.

INADEQUACY A lack of confidence and self-worth.

INTIMATE A closeness between people.

INTIMIDATION To fill with fear.

JEOPARDIZE To put someone or something in harm's way.

MANIPULATION To influence skillfully but unfairly.

MISGUIDED Misled or mistaken.

PLACATE To pacify through suggestion or action.

PLATONIC A nonromantic friendship or relationship.

REINFORCEMENT The aiding of a cause through numbers.

SELF-RELIANCE The ability to carry on all necessary tasks in life by oneself.

THERAPEUTIC Treatment that cures or makes one feel better physically or emotionally.

VALIDATE To confirm the viability of an action or person.

WITHDRAWN Shy or unsociable.

FOR MORE INFORMATION

Battered Women's Justice Project
1801 Nicollet Avenue S.
Suite 102
Minneapolis, MN 55403
(612) 824-8768
Website: http://www.bwjp.org
This group promotes justice and safety for victims of intimate
 partner violence and their families.

Canadian Women's Health Network
419 Graham Avenue, Suite 203
Winnipeg, MB 43C 0M3
Canada
Website: http://www.cwhn.ca
This voluntary national organization advocates for women's
 health in Canada.

Center for Relationship Abuse Awareness
555 Bryant Street #272
Palo Alto, CA 94301
(650) 752-6768
Website: http://stoprelationshipabuse.org
This organization provides awareness and education for com-
 munities, schools, and young people in an attempt to take
 collective action against gender violence

Futures Without Violence
100 Montgomery Street, The Presidio
San Francisco, CA 94129
(415) 678-5500

FOR MORE INFORMATION

Website: https://www.futureswithoutviolence.org
This organization works to helps teens end dating abuse
  through program and policy development that spurs public
  action.

Kids Help Phone Canada
300-439 University Avenue
Toronto, ON M5G 1Y8
Canada
(416) 586-5437
Website: http://kidshelpphone.ca
This agency provides help around the clock for young people
  experiencing a wide range of issues.

National Coalition Against Domestic Violence
1 Broadway Street, B-210
Denver, CO 80203
(303) 839-1852
Website: http://www.ncadv.org
This organizations works to change public policy, increase
  understanding of domestic violence, and create programs in
  an attempt to establish a zero tolerance society for domestic
  abuse.

National Domestic Abuse Hotline
PO Box 161810
Austin, TX 78716
(800) 799-7233
Website: http://www.thehotline.org
This hotline is available twenty-four hours a day and provides
  confidential and free services to enable victims to find safety
  and escape abusive relationships.

National Network to End Domestic Violence
1325 Massachusetts Avenue NW
7th Floor
Washington, DC 20005-4188
(202) 543-5566
Website: http://nnedv.org
The NNEDV is dedicated to creating a social, political, and economic environment that would end violence against women.

US Department of Justice
950 Pennsylvania Avenue
Washington, DC 20530-0001
(202) 514-2000
Website: https://www.justice.gov/ovw
This government agency seeks to identify and prevent gender bias in law enforcement in responding to sexual assault and domestic violence.

WEBSITES

Because of the changing nature of internet links, Rosen Publishing has developed an online list of websites related to the subject of this book. This site is updated regularly. Please use this link to access the list:

http://www.rosenlinks.com/HCIH/abuse

FOR FURTHER READING

Anderson, Laurie Halse. *Speak.* New York, NY: Square Fish Books, 2011.

Canfield, Jack, Mark Victor Hansen, and Kimberly Kirberger. *Chicken Soup for the Teenage Soul: Love and Learning.* New York, NY: Back List LLC, 2012.

Covey, Sean. *The 7 Habits of Highly Effective Teens.* New York, NY: Touchstone Books, 2014.

Eastham, Chad. *The Truth About Breaking Up, Making Up, and Moving On.* Nashville, TN: Thomas Nelson Publishers, 2013.

Eastham, Chad. *The Truth About Dating, Love, and Just Being Friends.* Nashville, TN: Thomas Nelson Publishers, 2011.

Elliott, Susan. *Getting Past Your Breakup: How to Turn a Devastating Loss into the Best Thing That Ever Happened to You.* Boston, MA: De Capo Lifelong Books, 2009.

Fairweather, Lynn. *Stop Signs: Recognizing, Avoiding, and Escaping Abusive Relationships.* Berkeley, CA: Seal Press, 2012.

Fonda, Jane. *Being a Teen: Everything Teen Girls & Boys Should Know About Relationships, Sex, Love, Health, Identity & More.* New York, NY: Random House, 2014.

Holyoke, Nancy. *A Smart Girl's Guide: Surviving Crushes, Staying True to Yourself, and Other (love) Stuff.* Middletown, WI: American Girl, 2013.

Hunter, Joanna V. *But He'll Change: End the Thinking That Keeps You in an Abusive Relationship.* Center City, MN: Hazelden Publishing, 2009.

Levy, Barrie, and Patricia Occhiuzzo Giggans. *When Dating Becomes Dangerous: A Parent's Guide to Preventing Relationship Abuse.* Center City, MN: Hazelden Publishing, 2013.

Manecke, Kirt. *Smile & Succeed for Teens: A Crash Course in Face-to-Face Communications.* Milford, MI: Solid Press, 2014.

Waldal, Elin Stebbins. *Tornado Warning: A Memoir of Teen Dating Violence and Its Effect on a Woman's Life.* Carlsbad, CA: Sound Beach Publishing, 2011.

BIBLIOGRAPHY

Center for Relationship Abuse Awareness. "How to Help a Friend Who Is Being Abused." 2015. http://stoprelationshipabuse .org/get-help/how-to-help-a-friend.

Department of Health and Human Services. "Office on Women's Health: Violence Against Women. How to Help a Friend Who Is Being Abused." September 4, 2015. http://womenshealth .gov/violence-against-women/get-help-for-violence/how-to-help-a-friend-who-is-being-abused.html.

Eastham, Chad. *The Truth About Breaking Up, Making Up, and Moving On.* Nashville, TN: Thomas Nelson Publishers, 2013.

Fairweather, Lynn. *Stop Signs: Recognizing, Avoiding, and Escaping Abusive Relationships.* Berkeley, CA: Seal Press, 2012.

Girlshealth.gov. "Running Away." February 19, 2015. http:// girlshealth.gov/feelings/runaway/index.html.

Love Is Respect. "A Teen's Guide to Safety Planning." Retrieved March 2016. http://www.loveisrespect.org/pdf/Teen-Safety-Plan.pdf.

Metcalf, Eric. "Are You in an Abusive Relationship?" WebMD, August 8, 2011. http://teens.webmd.com/boys/features/ abusive-relationship-and-teens.

National Domestic Violence Hotline. "Get the Facts and Figures." Retrieved March 2016. http://www.thehotline.org/ resources/statistics.

The National Domestic Violence Hotline. "How Can You Help a Friend or Family Member?" Retrieved March 2016. http:// www.thehotline.org/help/help-for-friends-and-family.

Ray-Jones, Katie. National Domestic Violence Hotline CEO. Interview with author, March 25, 2016.

Start Strong Teens. 2016. http://startstrong.futureswithoutviolence
    .org.
Szabo, Liz. "Study: One in Five Teen Girls Victim of Dating
    Violence." *USA Today*, March 2, 2015. http://www
    .usatoday.com/story/news/2015/03/02/teen-dating-violence
    -study/24127121.
Teens Experiencing Abusive Relationships. "Cycle of Abuse."
    2007. http://www.teensagainstabuse.org/index.php?q=cycle.
Transition House. "Restraining Orders." 2015. http://www.
    transitionhouse.org/get-help/restraining-orders.

INDEX

A

absences from school/work, 11
abuse
  celebrities and, 20
  male victims of, 7, 42–43
  myths and facts about, 24
  statistics on, 5–6, 7, 42
  warning signs of, 5, 8–11
anger, 15, 16, 35
anxiety, 11

B

Brown, Chris, 19, 20
bruises, 11, 14

C

celebrities, abuse and, 20
Clothesline Project, 36
compromise, 26
confidence, loss of, 11
confidentiality/privacy, 12, 14
control/power, 8, 11, 12, 13, 21,
    22–23, 42
counselors/guidance counselors,
    5, 9, 13, 22, 30, 31, 35, 48
  questions to ask, 50–51
"cycle of abuse," 27–28, 30

D

depression/sadness, 11, 35
domestic violence agencies, 22,
    31, 38
"Don't Look Away" campaign,
    29

F

Futures Without Violence, 26

G

gossip, danger of, 12–13
guidance counselors/counselors,
    5, 9, 13, 22, 30, 31, 35, 48
  questions to ask, 50–51

H

Hyland, Sarah, 10–11

I

intimidation, 7, 9

J

judgment, 13, 15, 16, 22, 34

ABOUT THE AUTHOR

Martin Gitlin is an educational book author based in Cleveland, Ohio. As a newspaper journalist from 1991 to 2002, he won more than forty-five awards, including first place for general excellence from the Associated Press, which selected him as one of the top four feature writers in Ohio in 2002.

PHOTO CREDITS

Cover antoniodiaz/Shutterstock.com; p. 4 Mita Stock Images/Shutterstock.com; p. 8 Julia Milberger/Hemera/Thinkstock; p. 10 DFree/Shutterstock.com; p. 12 Photodisc/Thinkstock; p. 14 Cathy Yeulet/Hemera/Thinkstock; p. 17 PhotoAlto/Laurence Mouton/Getty Images; p. 18 Hero Images/Getty Images; p. 20 Newspix/Getty Images; p. 25 Nonwarit/Shutterstock.com; p. 28 Jupiterimages/liquidlibrary/Thinkstock; p. 31 Mattz90/Shutterstock.com; pp. 34–35 Paul Simcock/Stockbyte/Getty Images; p. 37 29september/Shutterstock.com; p. 39 Gawrav Sinha/E+/Getty Images; p. 43 KL Services/Radius Images/Getty Images; p. 46 Pamela Moore/E+/Getty Images; p. 50 Yellow Dog Productions/Iconica/Getty Images; cover and interior pages background images © iStockphoto.com/chaluk.

Designer: Brian Garvey; Photo Researcher: Sherri Jackson; Editor: Rachel Gluckstern